Caterpillars

By Theresa Greenaway

Photography by Chris Fairclough

RSVP
RAINTREE
STECK-VAUGHN
PUBLISHERS
A Steck-Vaughn Company

Austin, Texas

Published by Raintree Steck-Vaughn Publishers, an imprint of Steck-Vaughn Company.

Acknowledgments
Project Editors: Gianna Williams, Kathy DeVico
Project Manager: Joyce Spicer
Illustrators: Stuart Lafford and Stefan Chabluk
Design: Ian Winton

Planned and produced by Discovery Books

Library of Congress Cataloging-in-Publication Data
Greenaway, Theresa, 1947–
Caterpillars/by Theresa Greenaway; photography by Chris Fairclough.
p.   cm. — (Minipets)
Includes bibliographical references (p. 30) and index.
Summary: Provides information on the identification, life cycle, and habitats of caterpillars, as well as on how to collect and care for them as pets.
ISBN 0-8172-5585-0 (hardcover)
ISBN 0-8172-4209-0 (softcover)
1. Caterpillars as pets — Juvenile literature. 2. Caterpillars — Juvenile literature.
[1. Caterpillars as pets. 2. Caterpillars. 3. Pets.] I. Fairclough, Chris, ill. II. Title.
III. Series: Greenaway, Theresa, 1947–   Minipets.
SF459.C38G74   1999
638' .578139 — dc21   98-34068
CIP   AC

1 2 3 4 5 6 7 8 9 0 LB 02 01 00 99
Printed and bound in the United States of America.

Words explained in the glossary appear in **bold** the first time they are used in the text.

> # WARNING
> Some hairy caterpillars can cause unpleasant allergic responses, such as itchy rashes. Hairs can detach from the caterpillar and work their way into human skin. Children and adults should avoid touching all hairy caterpillars.

Contents

Introducing Caterpillars

Caterpillars make ideal pets. It is a lot of fun to watch them grow and change. Caterpillars are the **larvae** of butterflies and moths. You can look after them until they turn into adult insects.

A female butterfly or moth lays its eggs on a plant. When the tiny caterpillars are ready to hatch, they nibble their way out of their eggshells. First they eat their eggshells. Then they use their sharp jaws to eat plant leaves.

◀ Caterpillars, such as this swallowtail butterfly caterpillar, are simply eating machines.

All a caterpillar has to do is eat and avoid becoming another animal's meal. It takes anywhere from a few weeks to several months for a caterpillar to grow to its full size. It then becomes a **pupa**. This is the halfway stage between a caterpillar and a moth or butterfly.

A caterpillar's body

Caterpillars have long, tube-shaped bodies. Below their mouths are tiny **silk glands**. Just behind a caterpillar's head are three pairs of tiny **true legs**. Toward their back end, there are usually ten stumpy legs called **prolegs**.

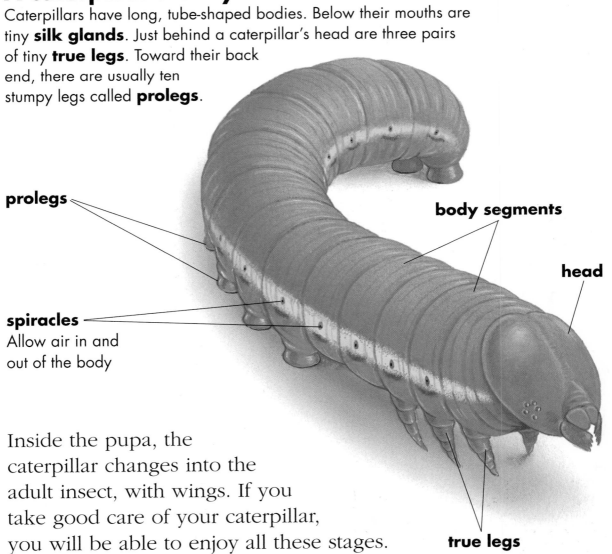

prolegs

body segments

head

spiracles
Allow air in and out of the body

true legs

Inside the pupa, the caterpillar changes into the adult insect, with wings. If you take good care of your caterpillar, you will be able to enjoy all these stages.

Finding Caterpillars

You can look for caterpillars anywhere that plants grow. Look carefully at the leaves of flowers, vegetables, and weeds. Good places to look are on **nettles**, cabbages, fruit trees, oak trees, and brambles.

Caterpillars try to hide from hungry birds, so finding them can take a while. As you are searching, think about the ways caterpillars protect themselves. They are very good at hiding.

Many kinds rely on blending in with the background. Some inchworms, for instance, look just like small, brown twigs.

◀ Look very closely, and you can see the inchworm on this branch.

Other kinds of caterpillars roll leaves around themselves. Then they wrap the leaves with silk to make tubes to live in.

Silky homes

Tent caterpillars use their silk glands to make themselves a silk tent. If you look in a wild cherry tree, you may find hundreds of tiny caterpillars sharing one tent.

Some caterpillars only come out at night, when most birds are asleep. Ask an adult to take a walk with you at night. Use a flashlight to look at some plants. You might be surprised at how much caterpillar activity you will find.

Caterpillar Collecting

Caterpillars are quite soft and can be damaged easily. You must handle them very gently, especially when they are young and tiny. You can move caterpillars by lifting them with a small, soft paintbrush.

Another way is to cut and collect leaves or twigs that have caterpillars on them. If you do this, you don't have to disturb the caterpillars at all.

Find as many kinds of caterpillars as you can. Put the different ones into separate jars or plastic containers with lids. Make sure you add fresh leaves from each caterpillar's own **food plant**.

Make small holes in the container's lid to let in air. The airholes also keep the container from becoming too damp.

Stick a label on each jar. Write on it where and when you found the caterpillar inside. This will help you identify your new pet later.

Hairy warning

Some kinds of caterpillars shed hairs that can cause rashes. So avoid touching them whenever possible. This brown-tailed moth caterpillar is very pretty, but its hairs will give you an itchy rash if they get stuck in your skin.

Identifying Caterpillars

When you have collected some caterpillars, it is time to identify them. Identifying caterpillars is not always easy, even for experts. Some are common garden pests, while others are very rare. You will need a book that has pictures of the caterpillars that live in your area.

If you cannot identify your new pets, write a description, or draw them in your notebook. Keep the caterpillars until they **pupate** and turn into butterflies or moths. It will be much easier to identify them. Next time you come across these caterpillars, you will know exactly what they are.

► If you know the name of the plant a caterpillar is eating, it may help you identify it. This large white butterfly caterpillar prefers to eat the leaves of cabbage or related plants.

Butterflies and moths are grouped together into families. Some of the most common butterfly families in North America are swallowtail butterflies, white and sulfur butterflies, brush-footed butterflies, and skipper butterflies. The most familiar moths are inchworm moths, emperor moths, hawk moths, and tiger moths.

Thousands of species

There are at least 125,000 known species of butterflies and moths. The two pictured below can be found in the United States and in Europe.

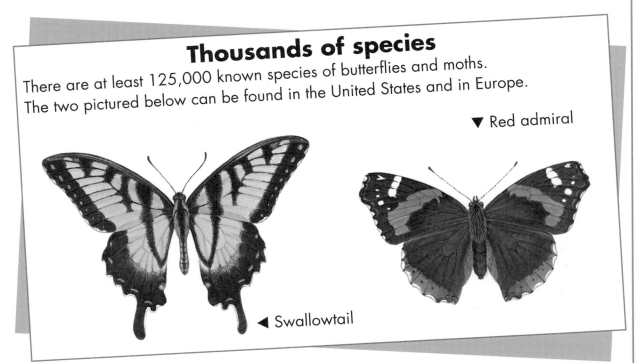

▼ Red admiral

◄ Swallowtail

Homes for Caterpillars

Your caterpillars will need a good home while you are keeping them. A small container with a few leaves is fine for little caterpillars. Tiny caterpillars can be kept in a plastic box or glass jar with a lid with airholes. But if you want to keep them until they change into butterflies and moths, you will need a bigger home.

Underground homes

Some caterpillars, such as this tomato hornworm moth larva, need soil to burrow into when they are ready to pupate. If you keep any kind of burrowing caterpillars, you will need to add a layer of soil to their home.

Line the container with paper towels. Put fresh leaves on the paper towels, and carefully move the caterpillars onto the leaves with a soft paintbrush.

lid

paper towel

fresh leaves

When the caterpillars are bigger, you can move them to a shoebox or larger plastic container covered with netting or wire mesh.

Another way for you to observe your minipets is by standing a caterpillar's food plant in a jar of water. Put cotton around the stems in the jar's neck to keep the caterpillars from falling down into the water. You can leave the jar outside. As long as a caterpillar has enough to eat, it will stay on the leaves.

Caring for Caterpillars

Caterpillars don't need much looking after. But you will have to give them plenty of fresh food, fresh air, and the right amount of moisture.

Caterpillars will die if they are too wet or too dry. Don't put them next to a heater, or anywhere cold and damp. Do not leave their home directly in the sunlight.

Breathing bodies

Can you see the **spiracles** on the side of this tobacco hornworm moth caterpillar?

Be sure to remove all wilted leaves and any caterpillars that die. It is also important to remove as many of the caterpillars' droppings as possible, using a paintbrush or small spoon.

Unless you clean the caterpillars' homes, mold will grow that could kill your pets.

Try to keep caterpillars in conditions as near as possible to those where they were found. Be very careful not to let caterpillars escape inside your home!

Feeding Caterpillars

Some caterpillars are very picky about what they eat. They will only eat one kind of leaf. Others are not nearly so fussy and will happily eat many different plants.

It is important to identify what caterpillars are eating when you find them.

▲ Woolly bear caterpillars eat many different leaves, from weeds to vegetables.

There may not be enough of the food plant to last while you keep your caterpillars. You will need to find more plants of the same kind before you run out of leaves.

You can also look in a caterpillar guide to see if there is something else they will eat. Any new leaves must be introduced gradually, before you have run out of the caterpillar's usual food. Otherwise, they might just stop eating.

Poisonous prey

Caterpillars of the monarch butterfly eat poisonous milkweed leaves. The caterpillar is not affected by the poison, which it stores in its skin. The colorful markings of the caterpillar warn birds that they will be sick if they eat it.

Tiny caterpillars need young, delicate leaves. As they grow, the caterpillars' jaws get stronger, and they can chew much tougher leaves. Caterpillars will not eat wilted or dying leaves, so you will need to replace these with fresh ones.

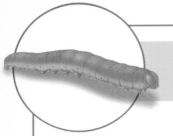

Watching Caterpillars

You can learn a lot about your minipets by watching them with a hand lens. You will soon see that caterpillars eat constantly. Do they all bite and chew in the same way? Can you see the caterpillars' jaws? These are the parts that actually cut into the leaves.

Watch how caterpillars walk along leaves and twigs without falling off. The front legs are used mostly to guide the caterpillar and to hold leaves for eating.

On each of the prolegs are tiny hooks. These grip onto the surface of the leaves so that the caterpillar does not fall.

▼ This tiger moth caterpillar is using its prolegs to grip tightly onto a branch.

Moving house

The bagworm caterpillar spins a silk case around itself, sticking in tiny pieces of plants as extra protection. It moves around with the bag sticking up behind it. The bag eventually becomes its cocoon.

As a caterpillar grows, its skin becomes too tight. The caterpillar **molts** to get rid of its outgrown skin. Watch your caterpillar for signs that it is ready to molt. If a caterpillar stops moving around and eating, it may be that it's just too big for its skin!

▼ The tight skin of a molting caterpillar splits to reveal a new skin underneath. Then the caterpillar wiggles out of the old skin and expands into the new, looser skin.

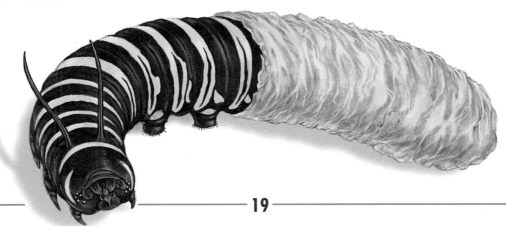

Growing Up

When it is fully grown, a caterpillar prepares to pupate. First it must find a safe place. Look in your caterpillar guide to see what your caterpillars will need for their pupa stage.

▶ Many moth caterpillars spin **cocoons** of silk to protect their chrysalises.

Pupa preparations

You may see your caterpillar attach itself to a leaf or twig. Its skin rolls back to reveal the pupa underneath. The pupa case hardens and protects the insect while it changes into an adult.

Some caterpillars pupate hanging on the twigs where they have been feeding. Others look for shady, sheltered spots. If your caterpillars are in a container, you will need to provide the twigs or shelter they need.

Caterpillars that pupate underground may move around in the dirt on the bottom of their container for several days before they settle down to pupate.

▼ When its wings have dried, this new butterfly will be ready to fly.

Once the caterpillar has found a safe place, its skin starts to split. This time, underneath the old skin is a pupa case. The pupa of a butterfly or moth is often called a **chrysalis**. Inside the chrysalis, the wingless caterpillar changes into the winged, adult insect. This can take anywhere from 10 days to many months. Then the pupa case splits, and the adult insect struggles out.

When Winter Comes

Surviving the winter can be hard for caterpillars. Many plants lose all their leaves, so there is no food. It is much too cold for caterpillars to move around. So how will your pets get through the winter?

▼ The giant silkworm caterpillar will spend the winter as a pupa in its cocoon.

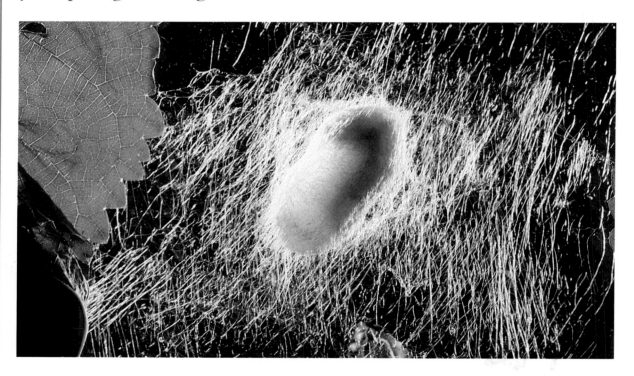

Many caterpillars never see winter. They hatch in the spring and turn into adult insects by fall. Others are fully grown caterpillars by late summer or fall, and pass the winter months as pupae.

Check your caterpillar guide to see what your pets will do in the winter. You may have caterpillars that will survive the winter by **hibernating**. Some hide away on their food plant. Others crawl underground. They stay there until the weather grows warmer. While they are hibernating, caterpillars do not move or eat.

Some butterflies that emerge in the fall will also hibernate all winter. But other butterflies **migrate**. As soon as fall arrives, they fly to warmer places. It is very important to release any butterflies you have raised if they need to migrate.

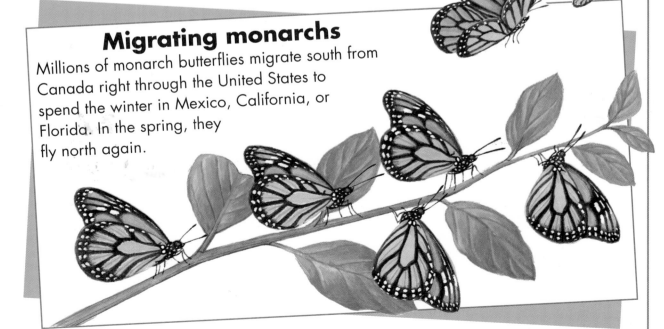

Migrating monarchs

Millions of monarch butterflies migrate south from Canada right through the United States to spend the winter in Mexico, California, or Florida. In the spring, they fly north again.

Keeping a Record

You can have a lot of fun studying caterpillars. It is a good idea to keep a scrapbook and write down everything you learn about your pets.

Paste in any pictures or articles that you find in magazines. Find out if there is a local club for butterfly and moth enthusiasts.

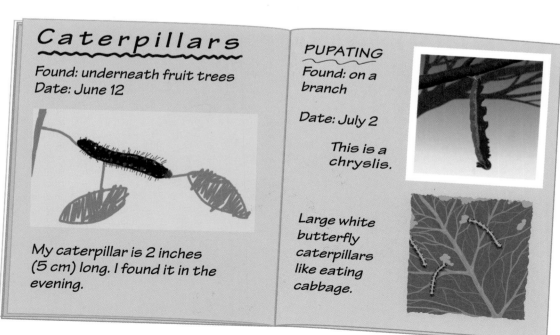

Caterpillars

Found: underneath fruit trees
Date: June 12

My caterpillar is 2 inches (5 cm) long. I found it in the evening.

PUPATING

Found: on a branch

Date: July 2

This is a chryslis.

Large white butterfly caterpillars like eating cabbage.

It is interesting to compare the life cycle of one kind of caterpillar with another. Make a note of what they eat, what they look like, and how they change as they grow larger.

Note the date that they pupate. Describe what the chrysalises look like, and if they change color just before hatching. Record when the adult butterflies and moths appear.

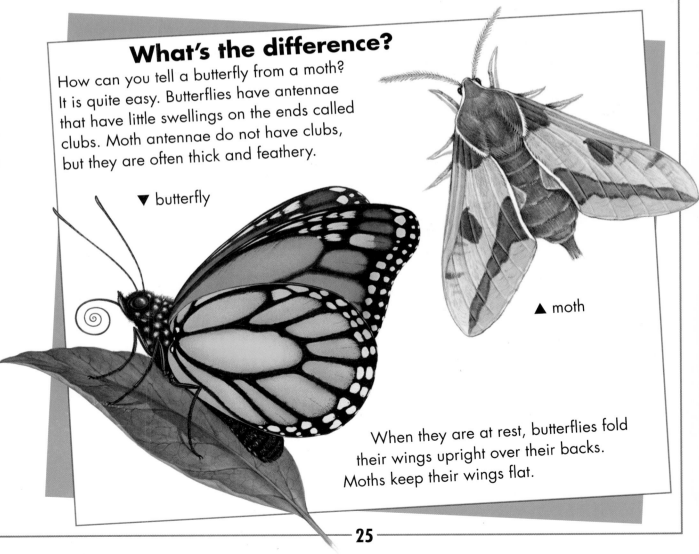

What's the difference?

How can you tell a butterfly from a moth? It is quite easy. Butterflies have antennae that have little swellings on the ends called clubs. Moth antennae do not have clubs, but they are often thick and feathery.

▼ butterfly

▲ moth

When they are at rest, butterflies fold their wings upright over their backs. Moths keep their wings flat.

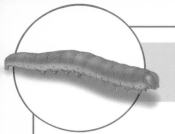

Letting Them Go

You may want to release your caterpillars after observing them for a short while, and before they pupate. If you decide to let your caterpillars go, make sure you put them back onto their food plant.

You can keep your pets until they turn into butterflies or moths. Releasing your very own butterflies or moths that you have raised from tiny caterpillars is a wonderful thing to do. If you try to keep butterflies or moths in cages, they will damage their lovely wings by trying to escape.

If you are lucky, you will see the adult insect crawl out of its chrysalis. Wait until its wings are dry and it is ready to fly before letting it go. You can let butterflies go during the day. But many moths only fly in the dark.

◀ A comma butterfly feeds on fleabane flowers.

Your pets will fly away to feed. Butterflies and moths feed on the sugary **nectar** they find in flowers. You could try growing flowers rich in nectar. This will encourage butterflies and moths to live and breed in your neighborhood. Then you will be able to find more caterpillars.

Caterpillar Facts

Caterpillars that can defend themselves are usually brightly colored. They may have an unpleasant smell or taste, or hairs that can sting. Their bright markings warn predators to leave them alone.

▼ Cinnabar moth larva

This means they can feed out in the open instead of hiding, like most other caterpillars do.

◄ Monarch butterfly larva

Asian silkworm caterpillars spin large cocoons. Over 4,000 years ago, people in China discovered how to turn these into silk cloth. All the silk made today still comes from these silkworms.

When the gumleaf skeletonizer caterpillar molts, its old skins stay stuck, piling up on its back. The caterpillar uses its molted skins as a strange form of defense.

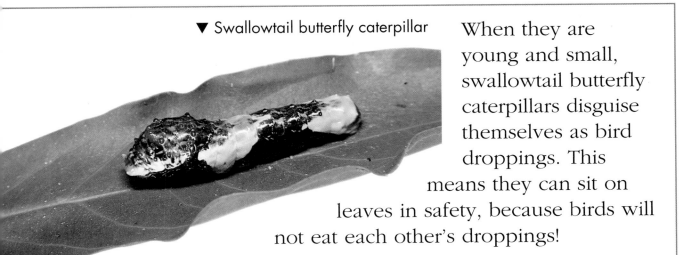

▼ Swallowtail butterfly caterpillar

When they are young and small, swallowtail butterfly caterpillars disguise themselves as bird droppings. This means they can sit on leaves in safety, because birds will not eat each other's droppings!

Not all caterpillars eat leaves. Clothes moth caterpillars eat wool or velvet. Caterpillars of harvester butterflies eat aphids and leafhoppers.

The caterpillars of the European large blue butterfly are captured by ants and carried into the ants' nest. These caterpillars give a sugary liquid that the ants like to eat. In exchange, the caterpillars eat some of the ant larvae.

▼ Caterpillar of large blue carried by ants

Further Reading

Legg, Gerald, and David Salariya. *From Caterpillar to Butterfly*. Franklin Watts, 1998.

Merrick, Patrick. *Caterpillars*. Child's World, 1997.

Morgan, Sally. *Butterflies, Bugs, and Worms*. Larousse Kingfisher Chambers, 1996.

Pascoe, Elaine. *Butterflies and Moths*. Blackbirch, 1996.

Savage, Stephen. *Butterfly* (Observing Nature series). Austin, TX: Thomson Learning, 1995.

Glossary

Cocoon A case of silk spun by the caterpillar.

Food plant A plant upon which caterpillars feed.

Hibernate To spend the winter resting in a sheltered place.

Larva The wingless, often wormlike form of a newly hatched insect.

Migrate To travel a long distance to spend part of each year in a different climate.

Molt To shed the tough outer coat, or exoskeleton.

Nectar A sweet liquid found in many flowers.

Nettles A plant with sharp or prickly hairs that give a sting when touched.

Prolegs The stumpy back legs of caterpillars.

Pupa (chrysalis) The stage in some insects' life cycle in which the larva changes into a winged adult.

Pupate When the larvae of some groups of insects stay still inside a case while turning into an adult.

Silk glands Tiny organs that squeeze out droplets of liquid. The caterpillar pulls these into threads of silk.

Spiracles Breathing holes or vents along each side of the caterpillar's abdomen.

True legs Three pairs of jointed legs at the front end of a caterpillar.

Index

The publishers would like to thank the following for their permission to reproduce photographs:
cover (caterpillar) © Kim Taylor/Bruce Coleman, 4 Bruce Coleman, 6 Robert A. Lubeck/Oxford Scientific Films,
7 Jack Dermid/Bruce Coleman, 9 G.E. Hyde/Frank Lane Picture Agency, 11 Hans Reinhard/Bruce Coleman, 12 Donald
Specker/Oxford Scientific Films, 14 Silvestris/Frank Lane Picture Agency, 16 Alvin E. Staffan/Oxford Scientific Films,
17 David Wrigglesworth/Oxford Scientific Films, 18 J. Brackenbury/Bruce Coleman, 19 Peter Davey/Bruce Coleman,
20 G. E Hyde/Frank Lane Picture Agency, 21 & 22 Kim Taylor/Bruce Coleman, 27 Larry Crowhurst/Oxford Scientific Films,
29 Marie Read/Bruce Coleman